Carnaval

Brazilian Nights

Love Wild

Bibliografische Information der Deutschen Nationalbibliothek:

Die Deutsche Nationalbibliothek verzeichnet diese Publikation in der Deutschen Nationalbibliografie; detaillierte bibliografische Daten sind im Internet über http://dnb.dnb.de abrufbar.

Printed and published by: BoD -
Books on Demand, Norderstedt
ISBN: 978-3-7543-1891-1

"I know it's very loud." Michael's airbnb host, Ana, screamed on his ear over the bustle of the street party goers and the *trio elétrico* playing the traditional Carnaval beats, the *marchinhas*. "But that's the fun of it." She smiled, raising her neon green hard plastic cup in cheers.

He could barely hear himself when he spoke to her, and someone bumped into him every second or so, dancing or moving through the crowd. There were thousands of bodies packed together in the Rio streets, celebrating the national, cultural event that was the Brazilian Carnaval. Michael, a certified introvert who bristled when his personal space was breached by anyone but close friends, was having the time of his life. There was a good chance he had never touched so many strangers at once. And he went to the Superbowl once.

He had to place his mouth close to her ear in order to be heard.

"I might go deaf tonight." He laughed. The cheap alcohol he and Ana had been drinking for the past few hours had already loosened his inhibitions, making the world seem like a more relaxed, happier place.

It would have been better if his host, and now friend, wasn't stopped every two steps by a cheerful celebrant, who would speak in her ear in Portuguese and occasionally proceed to kiss her. Full, French-kissing. Michael would turn slightly to give them privacy, but he was hesitant of being lost in the crowd, so he had to stay near. Ana had explained it to him: in general, Brazilians were not too picky about kissing people, at least if compared to Americans. During Carnaval, that inhibition was lowered even further, and there was close to no ceremony needed before a few pecks were exchanged.

"My record was on the closing night of the 2016 Carnaval." She told him with great pride, early in their acquittance. "16 hotties smooched in a single evening. I could have gone higher, of course, but I have standards!"

There were a few ladies who had approached Michael already, though it seemed like men were expected to do the prompting there as well. He politely declined the advances, as none of them particularly caught his attention. As immersed as he was in the contagious feeling of the party, trading saliva with complete strangers was not exactly a turn on for him.

"You just need to drink more." Ana consoled him, as soon as he shared his thoughts on the subject.

She treated his unwillingness to partake on the uninhibited sexuality flowing all around as something to be fixed. As he watched her abandon herself fully to the party – free in a way Michael suspected he would need at least a few strong hallucinogens to achieve – it became clear to him that she might have had a point. Being able to unwind and let yourself be led wherever Rio's street Carnaval took you seemed to grant people a higher experience, one unlike any other. If one survived the dangers involved – Michael's brain screamed a somewhat gruesome list of them repeatedly during those first few forays into the packed streets – it seemed like whatever was on the other side was worth it.

"We are meeting one of my friends tonight!" Ana yelled at him, as soon as she said goodbye to her latest kissing partner. That one had been a tall brunette dressed up as Wonder Woman. If Michael watched this time, instead of turning around, no one would judge him for it. "She's waiting by the street corner, let's go."

The place she pointed at as she spoke had to be no more than twenty feet back. It still took the two of them over ten minutes to reach it, as they had to force their way through the crowd in the opposite direction. Everyone was following the *trios elétricos*, which were big trucks with a stage on top from which the night's band played music at deafening decibels. Trying to go against the flow was a true challenge. Ana ignored Michaels reluctance to make skin contact and pulled him by the arm, her grip tight. Good thing she did, or they would have been separated within two minutes.

They finally stepped out of the denser crowd. Michael took a deep breath, relishing in the break from the overheated bodies.

"*Finalmente, mulher!*" A petite blonde greeted Ana, as soon as they reached their destination. Pecks on the cheek were traded then, one for each side, as was the custom in this region. "*Que demora, ein. E quem é o gostoso?*"

The two of them smirked at him, and Michael fidgeted, uncertain. It was disconcerting to not understand what people were saying around him, but Ana didn't allow him to dwell on his awkwardness.

"This is Michael." She introduced him in English, for his benefit. He was pulled closer by the elbow. "He's a *gringo*, from California." He nodded in confirmation.

To both his relief and disappointment, the blonde girl extended a hand for him to shake instead of going for the far more intimate face kisses most women there had greeted Michael with. She seemed to understand the cultural differences automatically and adapt herself to them. As amazing as his experience in Brazil had been so far, Michael was appreciative of her gesture.

"I'm Maria Luiza, but you can call me just Luiza. It's nice to meet you." She introduced herself. Her voice was warm and friendly, like most people he had met on this trip, but her accent was by far the smoothest he has heard here. Had he met her at a bar in LA, Michael would have had a hard time telling where she's from.

"Wow, your English is great." He complimented, earnestly.

"Thanks." She responded, not clarifying why a Brazilian young woman spoke a foreign language so well.

"Should we go back in again?" Michael asked them, both uncertain and excited at the perspective.

Ana wasn't listening anymore. She had her tongue down what must have been stranger number 7 that night. The 2016 record was broke that year. Luiza smiled at their friend's shenanigans. The expression made her seem prettier, somehow, and Michael did his best not to stare.

"So, what brings you here?" The blonde started conversation while they waited for Ana.

"It's on my bucket list. I've always wanted to come to Carnaval." Michael responded, honestly.

"Really? That's cool. Are you here alone?" Even though her tone was casual, Michael couldn't help the excitement that surged in him at the thought that she might have been asking for other reasons.

"Yeah, just me." He paused, thinking on what to say next. "What about you? Do you live here?"

Luiza nodded.

"My family lives in a small town about an hour away, but I moved here around five years ago." She clarified.

Ana pulled away from her latest conquest, and waved him goodbye as she walked closer to Michael and Luiza. Her smile was wide and utterly shameless.

"That one was a good kisser." She laughed. "Come on, let's get back to the party!"

Led by their team captain, Michael and Luiza made their way into the thick of the crowd again. There was definitely something to be said about the feeling created by the collective carefree cheerfulness. Though Michael was tipsy, he was nowhere drunk enough to generate that amount of euphoria. But the horde seemed to bring it out of him. He was a terrible dancer, yet he did his best to *samba* along with Ana while Luiza laughed. They meet strangers, not all of them interested in kissing or a romantic pursuit, and made instant friends of them. At one point, Luiza, Ana and a few other women opened a circle and had an impromptu dancing competition. The style they used must have been *samba*, as he never saw anything like it anywhere else. It was all feet and legs moving, hips swaying sensually, and wide smiles for the audience.

When it' was Luiza's turn, Michael was hypnotized. She moved like her body was made for it, balancing on top of her very high heels effortlessly, cheered on by the audience. She didn't win, and Michael didn't understand the criteria enough to be able to say why. Her dancing had been one of the most enticing things he had ever seen. On an impulse brought by a second neon-green cup of cheap alcohol, he told her his thoughts.

"You were amazing." It was nice to have the excuse to be so close to her, as he needed to speak right on her ear to be heard.

"Thanks." Her smile was brilliant, but there was a shy edge to it. Not coyness, but genuine insecurity.

"No, really. I couldn't stop watching you." He confessed.

Luiza grinned. The expression was bright, and she looked extra gorgeous with it. Michael felt his heart beat speed up. Before he could overthink what to do or say next, however, the song changed. Luiza jumped up and down in place, excited.

"I love this song!" She held on to his arms as she began to dance.

Michael was acutely aware that he was a terrible dancer even back home, where he knew what to do and expect. Right there, right then, he had no hope of being good, and he discovered that he didn't care. All that mattered was the rhythm of his body moving against Luiza's, the flowery, sweet smell of her hair when she turned around and pressed back against him. It became easier and easier to lose himself to it, and the drinks Ana kept bringing to the two of them only added to that. They were all sweet and mild, or so he thought, up until the alcohol hit his system like a bus with no driver.

The world swayed on its axis, and his groin tightened with the need to urinate. He excused himself to Luiza, not thinking clearly anymore. He found a bush to relive himself in, then turned back to the throng of people to find that he had utterly and completely lost the two women he had been partying with.

He was also too drunk to care about it as much as he should. Mostly, Michael was unhappy to have lost Luiza, so he walked around the sweaty, moving bodies, attempting to spot her. Suddenly, he was pulled by his arm. When he turned to look, it was a woman he has never seen before. She was tall, and older looking, but pretty.

She smiled at him and, without exchanging any words, went in for a kiss. Her lips tasted sweet from her lip gloss, and Michael forgot what he had been doing, allowing the moment to happen. When they parted, she spoke. He didn't understand a single word of it.

"Hey… sorry, I didn't get that." He said.

"*Ah, um gringo. Não fala português, não?*" She seemed surprised, but not put-upon.

"I don't speak Portuguese, sorry."

"*Tudo bem, querido. E se a gente for para outro lugar juntos?*" Her grin had a sensual, dangerous edge to it. Were Michael in a better state, he would have known what she was saying without the need for a translation. As it was, he was just confused.

But before he could go along with something he was far too drunk to think through, a familiar voice called.

"Michael! I found you, finally." Luiza made her way out of the crowd to stand right by his side.

She put her arm over his shoulders with possessive familiarity, glaring at the stranger Michael had been talking to.

"Luiza, it's so nice to see you again." Michael smiled, dopily. She looked even prettier now than he remembered her being. When he swayed on his feet, she kept him upright. "I got lost."

"I know, sweetie. It's okay." She reassured him.

Before Michael could continue the conversation, the strange woman said something in Portuguese, her tone harsh. Luiza responded similarly, and their interaction continued for a few more moments, until at last the stranger rolled her eyes and walked away.

"You just saved me, so I guess you're a knight in shining armor." He told Luiza. "But you look a lot more like a Princess, or a Queen." He hiccupped.

To his reward, Luiza seemed amused and flattered by his words. But she let them slide without a direct response.

"I've lost Ana, but she knows better than to drink herself stupid in here." She shook her head, making the pretty golden waves of her hair bounce. Michael stared. "You, my friend, are three sheets to the wind, as Americans would say." Though her tone was admonishing, she didn't seem angry.

"I'm sorry." Michael apologized anyway, because his brain had been reduced to 'if girl pretty, make her happy' state.

"Come on, I live close by, you can sleep this off at my place." Luiza reassured him.

She walked, hand holding onto his tightly, and Michael followed obediently. Luckily, he didn't feel sick yet, and they were able to escape the crowd and make their way through slightly less full streets. Luiza walked fast and sticked to the well-lit sidewalks.

"You're lucky I found you." She told him, shaking her head. "This is not a great night to get mugged, buddy. The police will be overwhelmed. You might have also gotten yourself sexually assaulted, if it weren't for me." She smiled, but it was clear she was only half-kidding.

Exposed to the chilly night air and away from the energy of the party, Michael's mind had cleared considerably.

"I don't think that would have happened..." He protested.

Luiza shrugged in response.

"Good thing we will never know." She stopped by the dark entrance of one of the buildings in the street. "We are here."

Michael followed her inside and up what felt like an unending number of flights of stairs. She explained that she lived on the highest floor, because it was both safer and quieter. But as there were no elevators, getting there demanded a considerable amount of stairs-climbing.

"Saves me from having to pay for a gym membership." She joked. Michael couldn't fault her logic, especially since his brain wasn't working well enough to figure out anything more complicated than a faucet.

He would like to say that they got to her place, got a drink and talked about something, getting to know one another. His attraction to her was glaring, so she probably was aware of it after all. But the truth wase, they walked inside her small studio apartment, and Michael was ready to collapse on the first soft surface he saw. It happened to be the couch. His exhaustion and inebriation caught up to him in devasting fashion. However, Luiza gently to maneuvered him back to his feet and to a different direction, pushing him along until they were standing inside her bedroom. She gave him a small shove towards the bed, and he fell right into it.

"I will get you water. Then, you should sleep."

If she did as promised and got him that water, Michael didn't stay awake to find out.

His dreams were vivid and disjointed. A female form dancing in the middle of the ocean, waves swelling around as she moved, languid and strong at the same time. Michael felt like there was something he should do, or as if he had forgotten an important piece of information. Not even the dancing or the rhythm of the sea calmed him down. He startled himself awake sometime in the early morning, fully expecting to be in some curb, snoring away his drunkenness. But there was a soft mattress under him, and he could hear light, slow breathing by his side.

He was also painfully sober, and the memories of the night returned slowly and painfully.

"I guess she did bring the water, after all." He whispered to himself, taking the full glass he found on the bedside table and gulping its contents in a few seconds.

That was when Michael really looked around the room, eyes adjusted to the darkness. He could see the shapes of the furniture, a desk, a wardrobe, the door. Most importantly, the slumbering form on the other side of the double bed. Luiza, the woman he met just the night before, who likely saved him from getting into more trouble than he could handle. There was a fiery energy to her, mingled with a mysteriousness that had drawn him in immediately. Right then, as she slept, it was gone. In its place there was the form of a young woman, peaceful and trusting. She looked so very small, curled up on the very edge of the bed, the covers trapped under her body.

Michael did his best to be quiet as he got up and went to use her bathroom. His mouth felt fuzzy and gross, and he had to drink more water in order to curb the headache he could already feel forming on his temple. As he managed to get out of the bed without disturbing her, he seemed to be successful. He used Luiza's toothpaste and mouthwash, hoping she wouldn't mind, and drank as much water as he could stomach. He stepped out of the bathroom feeling like a new man, and was met with the sight of Luiza sitting up on the bed, disheveled and sleepy.

"Sorry, I didn't mean to wake you up." He tried not to wince. She had proven herself a good friend and he wanted nothing less than to inconvenience her.

Michael also couldn't help but notice that she looked downright adorable, as she slowly blinked herself awake.

"You worry too much." She mumbled, brown eyes focused on him. "Come back to bed."

"I can sleep on the couch. Thank you for taking me in, you really don't need to do anything else."

Luiza rolled her eyes at him, and Michael would have felt a little offended if she weren't so cute doing it.

"Get in. I'm the host, so you do as I say." She patted the space by her side.

Michael couldn't help the smile that spreads on his face.

"I don't think that's how it works..." He said, yet he moved to obey her. "Hosts don't get to boss their visitors around."

She smiled playfully at him.

"It's a Brazilian custom. The host has to be in charge, it's a whole thing." She explained, nodding along to emphasize the credibility of her words. "Come on, get under the covers."

She was insistent, and he was weak. So, he obeyed, walking back to her and slipping under the covers as instructed. He was sure it would be awkward, laying on the bed of someone he had only just met. But Luiza didn't seem bothered by the situation in the least. She turned around, and he felt her body relax on the mattress. Michael stared at the ceiling for a few minutes, sure that he wouldn't be able to fall asleep. He was out before he even noticed that it was happening.

There was something soft against his cheek. He felt it move higher, press closer, accompanied by the low sound of a sigh. Michael opened his eyes to find the room painted with the warm, yellow glow of the morning sun. There was a face above his, rosy lips pulled into a smile as she looked down at him.

"Good morning, sleepy." Luiza's eyes were puffy, letting him know she had just woken up herself. There was no makeup he could see on her face, not even the marks of whatever was leftover from the night before, so she must have at least gone to the bathroom before waking him up with a kiss on the cheek.

"Hi." He said, taking a moment to go back to himself. Pushing his body up, he sat on the bed. "Did you just kiss my cheek?"

"You're so cute when you're asleep." She defended herself. "It was entirely platonic, I promise."

"That's a bummer." Michael responded, smiling. Luiza rewarded him with a surprised grin.

"So, would you like some breakfast?" She got up from the bed, walking to her dresser to tame her wild, blonde strands with a comb.

"Sure." Michael got up as well, walking into the bathroom. "Do you have coffee?"

He could hear Luiza's affronted gasp from where he stood in front of the sink.

"You really know nothing about this country!"

Breakfast was a surprisingly comfortable affair. Luiza was generous with both her food and her laughter. She asked him questions about his life freely, and it felt like her interest was sincere, not motivated by other things. He would be lying, however, if he said he wasn't looking at her shapely legs under her oversized sleepshirt every opportunity he got, whenever she was up and moving around kitchen.

"When are you going back home?" Was one of the questions she posed, as they collected the dirty plates and put them on the sink.

"Tomorrow." Michael answered, regretfully.

"Really? Already?" She seemed disappointed. Leaning on the counter, a thoughtful look was on her face.

"Yes, unfortunately." He responded.

Michael knew it was the time to take his leave. She had been an incredibly solicitous, gracious host. Likely saved him from a mugging or something worse the night before. And he probably would never see her again in his life. It wasn't like a trip to Brazil was cheap, and for her, traveling to the USA would be even more unlikely. If only they had enough of a relationship to justify it… but after so little time together, it wasn't a possibility. Despite what Hollywood movies would like people to believe, falling in love during vacation is not really financially feasible.

"I'm about to do something I thought myself above doing." She told him. There was a glint he couldn't put his finger on in her eyes.

"Be my guest." He said, curious.

Luiza took a step towards him, then another, until she stood mere inches away from him. She stared up into his eyes, and Michael's heart caught up to the moment, jumping right into beating its way out of his chest. Metaphorically.

"You're leaving soon, and I *really* wanna fuck you before you're gone."

His brain stuttered to a halt. Completely. But Luiza didn't need him to take charge. Going on to her tiptoes, she pushed her lips against his, closing her eyes. The kiss was unhurried, languid like a post-party morning, and it tasted like the sweet pastry she had for breakfast. It had a girl's name… *carolinas*, that was it. They were little pastries filled with *doce de leite* and covered with chocolate. Michael ate five of them, much to his host's amusement.

Regardless of his faltering brain, Michael's body knew what to do. He kissed her back, savoring the feel and taste of her. His hand held her waist, pulling her small body closer until they were pressed together. Her clothes were so very thin that he could feel the softness of her breasts against his chest, the perfect curve of her hip under his hand. His brain only got back to work when she pulled away, lips shimmering with wetness, slightly reddened from the kiss.

"God, you're gorgeous." He told her, because it was true.

She smiled, her hand holding his face. There was something about being touched by a woman with such care that drove a shiver down Michael's spine.

"You're beautiful, too." She landed a peck on his lips. "Do you want to do this?" A kiss was pressed on his jaw.

Before he could overthink the situation or do anything to hurt the experience they could have together, Michael decided to let his uncertainty go and simply enjoy what was in front of him. He took action. She was small and light, so taking her into his arms on a bridal carry was a simple task. She squeaked in surprise, but even that sound was feminine and pretty.

"Hey!" Her protest was short-lived, as the apartment was tiny, and in just a few moments they were in her room, in front of her bed.

"Sorry." He apologized insincerely, smiling playfully as he deposited her on the still undone bed.

Luiza was an interesting mix of self-assured and timid, open and mysterious. Right then, she was sensual as well, and not afraid to play with it. She leaned back on her elbows on the bed, her legs parting to expose the cotton strip of her underwear that was the only thing shielding her sex from his gaze.

"Come here." She invited him.

Michael didn't need to be told twice. Divesting himself of his shirt took a second, and then he was on her. They tussled and rolled together, kissing and exploring each other's body, the relaxed languidness of the morning forgotten in favor of servicing the heat of their desires.

"You smell so good." He told her, burying his nose on that smooth nook between her shoulder and her neck, where the scent of her skin was both strongest and most delightful. There was something flowery, something sweet, and something spicy to it. A heady concoction that made his mouth water.

"You do too." She confessed. "Logic says you shouldn't, because we partied too hard yesterday. But you do." As if to prove the veracity of her words, Luiza spread wet kisses down his face and neck.

Her hands were everywhere on him. All that he did, she responded with full intensity and then some. It was not the level of engagement he had found with most of his previous partners, and it was driving him a little out of his mind. His erection was hard and throbbing, pressing against the fly of his shorts uncomfortably, and when Luiza touched it over his pants, he could do nothing more than groan in pleasure. She undid his belt, brown eyes locked on his like the minx she was, and made the action of working his pants open into a seduction itself.

Her hands were small and delicate, and Michael got a rush out of watching them caress the obvious bulge on his underwear. He was happy to notice that she seemed pleased as well. She seemed to enjoy the teasing and the anticipation as much as he did. Taking him by surprise, she leaned forward until she could mouth his cock over his underwear, wetting it with saliva, her eyes closed in enjoyment.

"Fuck, Luiza." He put a hand on her hair, not to direct or control her actions, but because he simply couldn't resist the urge to keep touching her.

"Don't rush me. We will fuck a few minutes." She answered, saucily. Michael smiled, but it slid from his face when she nibbled on him lightly, making his covered cock twitch.

"You're the boss." He let her know, to her obvious satisfaction.

Luiza explored him at her own pace, spreading generous, wet kisses on his member, nosing him through the under-wear. When she pulled it down, she did it with her teeth, and Michael felt like he must have been dreaming it was such a perfect, incredibly arousing moment. Something straight out of his most shame-less fantasies.

"Luiza…" Her name became a mantra, the one word that mattered as she effectively drove him out of his mind.

She licked him obscenely, from root to tip, not breaking eye contact for a moment. Swirling her tongue around the head, she fondled his testicles with one hand and held his cock in place with the other. Michael was restless, impatient, but Luiza ignored his yearning stares and pleading words easily. She followed her own whims, sucking on his cock at a leisure place, pumping the length she couldn't take in her mouth with one hand, attending to his balls with the other. It felt incredible. But also like she could keep building him like that for hours, without ever doing enough to let him come.

"Ready to see a really neat trick?" She asked, right at the point where Michael was mostly just sweating, not capable of much thought any longer.

He nodded.

"Yes, please."

Her smirk was devious, downright danger-ous. She put her hands on his hips and, closing her plump lips around his cock, be-gan sliding his length inside her mouth. Mi-chael was perfectly still, feeling a like the air had been knocked out of him. He was a fairly big dude, and until then, no woman had ever been able to deepthroat him. Luiza frowned as she swallowed more and more of him, her jaw widening to its maxi-mum to accommodate his thickness, but she forged on regardless. Michael's hand on her hair was light, but he buried his fin-gers on her blonde strands, just feeling the movement of her against him.

"Fuck!" He cursed loudly when he felt him-self hit the back of her throat, her button nose pressed against his pelvis. He was fully inside, at last.

She swallowed and his balls clenched, ready to shoot. Michael had to close his eyes and concentrate, or he would have come right then, after barely a minute of getting to enjoy the most expert blowjob he ever had the pleasure of receiving.

"You're so good, baby." He told her, pushing the hair out of her face as she worked his length in and out of her mouth. "It feels amazing."

Her only answer was a humming sound that made Michael lose his voice for a long moment. The vibrations were much stronger on the back of her throat, where his cock now reached, than he would have felt on her mouth or lips. He couldn't quite describe his level of disappointment when she let him slip away.

"Do you want to come like this?" She jerked him as she spoke, as to not let his excitement wither. As if it could.

Michael had to think about it, very hard. He certainly did want to come like that. The idea of shooting his load so deep in her throat she wouldn't even taste it had definitive appeal. But he also wanted to fuck her pussy. Maybe there was a compromise to be made.

"I want you to come on my cock first." He told her, sincerely. "But after, yes. If you're okay with that?"

She squeezed his member a little tighter, pumping it still.

"Sounds like a plan, big boy." She smiled, then slipped away, leaving the bed to open a drawer on her desk and look through it. "Ah, here we go." She declared triumphantly, holding up an unmistakable square little package.

Opening it with her teeth, she skipped back to him and slid it over his cock expertly. Michael was one of these men; each time she showed how comfortable she was with sex, his erection got a little harder. It was sexy and beautiful to see a woman like that. Stepping back from him, Luiza grabbed the hem of her shirt and pulled it over her head, exposing her body to him.

Her breasts were bigger than expected for a woman her size, round and firm as he discovered by touching them. There were lines on her skin revealing the chiseled muscles under, not exaggerated, but visible enough to let him know she had been lying the night before, and actually did spend some of her money on a gym membership. He could tell it was really working for her. But she was soft in all the right places, and the ratio between her waist and hips thoroughly pleased a deeply seated, animal part of his brain. It had something to do with it being a sight that she was a good child bearer, if his vague memories of biology class weren't mistaken, even though their encounter wasn't supposed to result in anything more than a few earth-shattering climaxes.

She slipped her panties down her legs, revealing that she was cleanly shaved. He stared. She was, perhaps, the most beautiful woman he had ever seen.

"Come here." He beckoned her, pushing his tangled underwear and shorts off, then sitting against the headboard.

Luiza positioned herself straddling Michael's legs, her wet pussy coming into contact with his cock. She took charge, taking him in hand and placing him against her entrance. She slowly allowed her body weight to pull her down, impaling her on Michael's length. It was a snug fit, and he held her by the hips, doing his best not to trust up. It felt so good that it was a herculean effort to not sink himself in her completely, to not pull down her small body so that it would encase him in its warm wetness.

"Oh, that's a stretch." She remarked, and there was humor in her words.

"Sorry." He apologized, fully aware that it could be uncomfortable for some women.

"Nah, I like it." She smirked, then kissed him, letting her bodyweight drive his cock deep within her at the same time.

They both groaned into the kiss. Michael could feel her slick dribbling down over his balls, and that was nearly as tantalizing as being buried inside of her. Wanting nothing more than for Luiza to get as much enjoyment out of this as he was, he slipped a hand between their bodies, quickly finding the hard nub of her clit and worrying at it. She held onto his arm, the clenching of her pussy around him also showing her appreciation.

She was as incredible at sex as she seemed to be at everything else. Moving slowly but firmly, she impaled herself on him again and again, with only the support of her strong legs and his hold on her waist. In this position, he could keenly feel her internal muscles clench with every movement, could watch her abs tense, could also kiss and lick at the exposed skin in front of him. He didn't waste the opportunity, taking a light brown nipple into his mouth, nibbling and sucking softly, then harder. She pulled his hair, spurning him on, and he changed breasts to give the other one equal attention.

Michael had been ready to come ever since she first slipped his cock inside her throat. His desire was no more manageable now, as he plundered her sweet insides, tasted her salty skin, and was kissed and touched by her in return. She was a through, generous lover, her hands sliding over his skin, getting to know him far more intimately than others had in the past. He flicked her clit faster, and after a few moments, he could feel her trembling on top of him.

"I'm going to come." She warned, eyes closed, mouth half-open to let out heaving breaths.

When she did, it was an unmistakable event. Her legs quivered, and he had to take over and thrust inside of her, as she seemed to lose her strength, her body falling heavy and lax on top of his. He turned them around without slipping from her body. Now on top, Michael could push himself inside of her, hard, work her through her orgasm and build himself higher for his. Before he could come, however, she pushed him away.

"...What?" He asked, confused, wondering if he did something wrong.

Luiza smirked and rolled her eyes.

"Didn't you want to come in my mouth?" She asked, much to his bewilderment.

She needed no prompting before she proceeded to free his painfully hard cock of the condom, and, kneeling on the bed, she shamelessly took him inside of her mouth just moments after he had been buried to the hilt in her sweet pussy. It was more than Michael could take. Guiding her head lightly, he pressed deeper in her, right until he was hitting the deepest spot he could. Right there, he came, so hard that his knees went weak and his vision was spotted for long seconds. He painted her throat white with his cum, and Luiza took it well, groaning in pleasure around his cock.

Michael immediately collapsed on the bed when he was done, feeling a little like he had been emptied through his balls. The world was softer and lighter, and a deep-seated languidness spread through his limbs. He fought it just enough to pull Luiza's body closer to his, pressing a grateful, caring kiss on her lips.

"That was incredible." He told her, nibbling on her plump lower lip just because he could.

"Incredible enough to convince you to stay a few more days?" She grinned, unapologetically.

Michael pretended to think about it.

"If you could make another demonstration, perhaps…?" He suggested.

To his delight, she laughed. Regardless of when he returned home, this indeed was one trip he would gladly, always remember.

TRANSLATIONS:

"*Finalmente, mulher!*" A petite blonde greeted Ana, as soon as they reached their destination. Pecks on the cheek were traded then, one for each side, as was the custom in this region. "*Que demora, ein. E quem é o gostoso?*" – "Finally, woman!" ... "You took so long. Who is the hottie?"

Gringo – Foreigner

"*Ah, um gringo. Não fala português, não?*" She seemed surprised, but not put-upon. – "Ah, a foreigner. You don't speak Portuguese?"

"I don't speak Portuguese, sorry."

"*Tudo bem, querido. E se a gente for para outro lugar juntos?*" Her grin had a sensual, dangerous edge to it. Were Michael in a better state, he would have known what she was saying without the need for a translation. As it was, he was just con-fused. – "That's okay, honey. What if we go somewhere else together?"